I0669801

John Stewart

The Tocsin of Britannia

With a novel plan for a constitutional army

John Stewart

The Tocsin of Britannia
With a novel plan for a constitutional army

ISBN/EAN: 9783337064662

Printed in Europe, USA, Canada, Australia, Japan

Cover: Foto ©Andreas Hilbeck / pixelio.de

More available books at **www.hansebooks.com**

THE

TOCSIN

OF

BRITANNIA:

WITH A

NOVEL PLAN

FOR A

CONSTITUTIONAL ARMY.

By JOHN STEWART,

THE TRAVELLER.

LONDON:

Printed for the AUTHOR, and sold by J. OWEN, No. 168,
Piccadilly, 1794.

Entered at Stationers Hall.

[PRICE TWO SHILLINGS.]

I MUST convert the preface to an incongruous ufe, and make it nothing but an infertion,
ferving to admonifh and recognize a clafs of
refpectable Patriots called Whigs, (forgot in
the body of the work) who ferve unintention-
ally as the edge of the wedge, or point of
the arrow, to the general clafs of revolutionifts; who, if left to themfelves, would
be blunted in power by their defperate circumftances and immoral characters, and their
jacobinical zeal would ferve only to alarm and
unite more firmly, the friends of Britain,
whofe ineftimable conftitution has been, and
ftill continues to be, the matrix of all focial
and moral perfectability.

2   I recommend

I recommend to all Britons fenfible of the perfectability of human nature, to turn all their attention to the temperate inftruction of the people, in the bofom of their families, to increafe thought, and to difcountenance all public affemblies, the fchools of fanaticifm, difcord, and revolution, tending to excite dangerous and precipitate action, the blight of all perfectability ; and let government form the ligatures of the patient, while philofophy conducts the knife of operation to couch the cataract of prejudice in the mental eye.

TOCSIN OF BRITANNIA.

THE awful importance of the prefent crifis diverts my mind from the profecution of a work of the moft profound theory, and calls imperioufly its attention to the practice of life, to difcover that delicate and precife line of conduct which is to guide political prudence, to preferve focial peace, the only medium of the exiftence or improvement of intellect, the fource of univerfal good.

I have travelled over the moft interefting parts of the globe, have obferved the miferable condition of human aggregation, formed by various modifications of civil power, but England is the only country in which I have met with moral union, exalting man to the moft elevated ftate of civilization.

B

By

By moral union, I mean the qualities of thought and reflection pervading a very confiderable mafs of the community, by which they are enabled to take a comprehenfive view of their political conftitution, to judge of it, not as a perfect immutable fyftem, but as an experiment of policy adapted to the prefent predicament of things, effecting not pofitive good, but fubftituting leffer to greater evil; and fo difpofed as to tend towards perfectability with a gradation fuitable to the improving progrefs of human intellect and the mutability of nature.

The great majority of the community, in whom thought and reflection have lefs influence, thefe form a factious leaven, whofe minds delighting in contingency, regard the revolutions of a country with the fame indifference as the revolutions of domeftic or individual life, and providing the day prefents a novelty of occurrences, they feel no apprehenfion of confequences deftructive of focial peace.

If we examine the conduct of the revolutionifts both in and out of parliament, they feem equally actuated by the common principle of contingency, and hoftility to fyftem; and though the ruins of civil fociety are ftill fmoaking after the conflagration of its edifice

in

in France, they ceafe not to throw around their inflammatory embers in this Ifland ; thefe, however, falling upon the non-combuftive matter of a thoughtful people, have no effect, while the more durable or hotter embers are extinguifhed by a Philofophic Jury, who know how to difcriminate the treacherous demagogue from the temperate and honeft reformer.

It is impoffible for a patriot Englifhman to read the fpeeches of parliamentary demagogues without feeling the moft violent fpafms of indignation. One of the moft thoughtlefs, and at the fame time the moft active, not long ago called upon the minifter to declare a rule or fyftem for war carried on againft a people who had deftroyed all rule and all fyftem, opening a vortex which threatened to ingulph all civilized fociety. The reply of the minifter fhewed that he poffeffed the characteriftic thought of the people he ferved, viz. " that national fafety could have no criterion but exifting circumftances ;" which wife anfwer feems drawn from a great moral axiom, that all principle muft contain the quality of * flexibility as to rule or capacity

* Among patriots, the word conftitution means nothing but falus populi fuprema lex ; but when they ufe it to the factious, it means fpecific rule or immutable law, a neceffary barrier to the fophiftry and fubtlety of crafty demagogues,

to

to adapt itself to predicament, but immutable as to end, the practical point of union of individual, and universal good, from which is projected the line of theory or perfectability; this point is to be discovered only by the exercise of thought and reflection investigating the most just and most general relations of things in interminable progression.

Not long ago, one of these thoughtless demagogues demanded an exposition of the quantity of arms this nation could furnish in case of an invasion; it was observed in reply, that this measure would give advantageous knowledge to the enemy; the motion however was still persisted in, because, forsooth, the character of a friend was implicated in the question, and national safety in the opinion of this demagogue was to cede to private affection.

·The whole tenor of the speeches of these dissipated, thoughtless demagogues, resembles more the pleadings of French Advocates than English Legislators; they are replete with chicane, built upon the inflexibility of * rule without respect to the end, with which doctrine they attempt to fix the mutability of nature, and like ignorant pilots would steer

* A man of principle pursues ever the same end, making flexible the rule of means; whereas knavery or ignorance substitutes the means for the end, and the rule for the purpose.

the

the veffel of the conftitution or ftate upon a direct though dangerous courfe, when winds, rocks, and fhoals of exifting circumftances demand a circuitous navigation to the harbour of fafety.

I do not mean to brand the whole of oppofition with a general mark of reprobation; I am convinced there are many well meaning members who are employed as honeft centinels over the balance of power, to prevent the dangerous and treacherous preponderancy of either of the three ftates, monarchy, ariftocracy, and democracy; and to preferve unimpaired the nice equipoife of the Britifh Conftitution, which folves the moft difficult of all problems, a fovereign people governed by a fovereign King, and holds out an incontrovertible teftimony of the progrefs of thought and reflection towards the climax of intellect in the Ifland of Great Britain.

I muft now addrefs myfelf with more particular and diffufe obfervations to the inferior clafs of demagogues. The titles of their different affociations I recommend as complete leffons for the conduct of their actions; had the fociety for conftitutional information been guided by their appellation, would they havehad the madnefs or folly to fend deputies from a drunken club

club to reprefent the majefty of the Englifh people? In Scotland, fhould they not rather have fent inveftigatory publications of the fyftem of government beft calculated to promote the progrefs of human intellect, addreffed to the intelligent and thoughtful part of the community, and not inflammatory penny publications to be forced into the hands of thoughtlefs plebeians, prone to precipitate action, which by deftroying fyftem muft caufe ever the retrogradation of intellect?

I recommend to thefe conftitutional inftructors to inform themfelves before they attempt to inform others, and when they have matured in their own focieties the Englifh characteriftics, thought and reflection, they may then diftribute them to others who would become affiliated members; and by thus increafing thought, the great and only fource of good, fentiment would be affimilated, and action would move in unifon upon the graduating line of perfectability. In the mean time I muft recommend the conduct of thefe affociated inftructors to the vigilance of a Britifh Jury, to check their inflammatory declamations and ambitious demagogues, and by a wife and philofophic verdict, mark the clear demarcation of fedition and inftruction.

There

There is another defcription of reformers, who have affumed the nobleft of all titles, viz. friends to the liberty of the prefs : this is however too thin a veil to caft the fhade of incognition over their notorious and inflammatory characters ; had their intention been conformable to their pretenfions, would they have been wholly 'occupied in the protection of bill ftickers and preachers of fedition? The true friends to the liberty of the prefs, are thofe only who confine it to inftruction and not inflammation, to thought and not to action, for the death of intellect is the natural confequence of the liberty of paffion, irreflection, and thoughtleffnefs. The liberty of the prefs muft be liable to the fame modifications as civil liberty.

It may be afked by fome well meaning members of thefe focieties, whofe benevolent difpofition has been duped by the fophiftry of demagogues, the infects of contingency, how are plebeian minds to be enlightened, if oral and fcriptural politics are not to be addreffed to them ? I anfwer, by Sunday Schools, by the writings of inquifitive philofophy calculated to prevent the precipitancy of action, by the pro and con confiderations of good and evil, infeparable from all inftitutions ; fuch reafoning repreffes represses passion, and increases thought and reflection, the true clue for graduating reformation which leads predicament on to perfectability.

I know some of these popular demagogues, and I am confident they are influenced by the base motives of personal vanity or personal interest; they pour out of their mouths a torrent of verbose nonsense in the midst of an assembly of irreflective youth, holding forth axioms formed and adapted to the primitive ages of an innocent and unpopulous world, which they recommend to the practice of a redundant and vitious population at the present æra. They would substitute the system of a sect for the policy of a nation which inveighs against murder, and opposes all criminal justice and national war; though without legalized murder there could be neither internal or external peace to society. The applauses of the majority, and the pockets of the minority of the audience, furnishes aliment to the unprincipled ardour of these demagogues, who are cautious to read and hear no discourse but what conforms to their habitual association of ideas, which is so tenacious that the sharpest wedge of doubtful wisdom has no power to separate.

The

The extreme paucity of numbers of these Jacobinical Reformers would have justified the most contemptuous silence ; the notice here taken of them was intended not to expose, but rather to instruct and instil into their minds of wit and levity, that proportion of thought and doubt which might render them naturally and civilly true British citizens.

If a proof was still wanting to corroborate the testimony of all mankind of the pre-eminency of thought and sagacity in the English Nation over all others, it has been discovered in the associations of the Yeomanry upon the breaking out of the war with France. They, with the most wonderful British intuition, took a full view of the moral and political crisis, and judged it to be a war of social existence. They discovered that the irreflective disposition of a nation depraved by despotism and superstition had no intention to reform, but to destroy civil order, and to scramble for property at the wreck, without considering that the scramble must be perpetuated 'till the most ferocious despotism should check it ; but, like the dog in the fable, they look only to get fat, and have not reflection enough to foresee the chain and the collar.

C

Let us take a concife view of the French Revolution, and we fhall find that in no one period was it directed by fyftem ; the forms of various conftitutions impreffed on parchment, but not the mind, had fcarce time to dry ere plebeian tumult made them a mockery. The prefent unparalleled energy of popular defpo-potifm, the pride of all Jacobins, muft fub-fide when the preffure of foreign hoftility which has created it fhall be removed. Is it poffible to give that country applaufe for the attainment of its prefent predicamental ener-gy ? It refembles the river difemboguing itfelf into the fea, and not the climax of graduated fyf-tem. In all defpotic countries, when the flood-gate of power is broken down, the want of civic knowledge in the people muft carry them downwards to the predicament of plebeian tumult, when law and order affording no protection, the mind overwhelmed with horror feeks fafety in the torrent of impulfe or popular frenzy, which, however energetic for the moment, muft in the end bring civil fociety to its diffolution.

It may be objected to the above mode of reafoning, that had France preferved conftitu-tional government, it could never have pro-cured an energy fuitable to its hoftile pre-dicament;

dicament ; if this be true, it tends to prove that the great mass of population was so corrupt, that like the confumptive patient, nothing but death could relieve it. The re-combinations of the politic body after dif-folution is as little fubject to calculation as the human body, whofe renovation of fenfation or life, muft be influenced by the exact quantity of good in exiftence at the moment of its death.

If it were poffible for the politic body to refift the evils of anarchy till education might produce a new generation, and reform the ig-norance in the great mafs of the aggregated people, anarchy would then be preferable to defpotifm ; but the agonies of anarchy are like thofe of the difeafe of the ftone, that calls upon the lithotomift of power for immediate cure or immediate diffolution.

If we look through all the works of nature, we find all the parts of exiftence organized into fyftem, whofe various capacities germinate into energy or perfectability ; fhould the pre-dicament of any one genus or fpecies affume an unaccommodating ftate, it muft draw upon itfelf either injury or diffolution, e. g. fhould fruit trees put forth their bloffoms in the midft of winter, the froft muft deftroy them ; fhould

a nation

a nation annul the evil fyftem of private property, or the fubjection of the minority to the
will of the majority of the community, called
Government, the fafety of furrounding nations, threatened by this new and unaccommodating predicament of revolution, would
oblige them to oppofe its progrefs. This
muft be done by a defenfive and not an offenfive fyftem. All violent and unfyftematic
revolutions by their internal concuffion would
fhake the cement out of the focial arch, and
caufe an inftant explofion of all its parts, if
fome external weight did not comprefs it.

The above reflection induces me to propofe
a plan of conduct to the confederate nations of
Europe in the prefent awful crifis. The offenfive
operations of war fhould be immediately put
a ftop to, and the following manifefto iffued
by the confederate powers :

In the facred name of univerfal good,
enlightened by the intelligence of progreffive
truth, fenfible that all modes of being are co-
exiftent and co-effential parts of one great integer, whofe energies operate in their refpec-
tive fpheres, communicable in motival influence
but incommunicable in motival direction, *

rendering

---

* The higher energies of nature, e. g. the fun may motivate
a man to walk out, but cannot direct his road. Again, the
head

rendering thereby every fphere the final and independant director of its own collective energies, to produce the greateft quantity of good to felf and nature in time and eternity, meafured by and related to the circumference of its own orbit; we, the Potentates of Europe, looking upon ourfelves as the central and protecting energy of the fenfitive fphere of exiftence, by this manifefto make known the purity of our intentions, and the expanfion of our confcience, enlightened by the knowledge of felf. Whereas the nation of France is overwhelmed by a moft dangerous anarchy, caufed and perpetuated by an irreflective, unprincipled, and ambitious faction, who have had cunning enough to infatuate a thoughtlefs multitude with the tenets of unmodified liberty and equality; tenets whofe leaven muft produce the moft incalculable fermentation by confounding the fool and the wife man, the individual and the public will; tenets, which have fo completely deftroyed all focial order by fubverting its bafe, viz. the fecurity of property and the fecurity of perfon; we judge it expedient for the protection of

Lead may motivate the attitude of the king; it is of the utmoft neceffity by its circulation to prevent an abufe of power. The faid reflective energies are inherent in all governments.

intellect, the high energy of this our fphere of exiftence, to form a cordon of armies upon the frontier of our own territories in the proximity of France, to repel all invafions of a diftempered and delirious people, and to be ready to ftretch out a protective hand to that remnant which may furvive the horrors of the prefent depopulating anarchy, and fhall call unequivocally for relief with fuch numbers as may affure fuccefs. We are determined to evacuate all our conquefts, and to avoid all conteft but what is purely defenfive; and as there is no authority in France to form a public will with whom treaties might be made, we are neceffitated to declare a peace, though we know no nation can hold peace with others that cannot firft give peace to itfelf, and fubjugated by a faction whofe power is fupported by war. We hereby make known to all interefted and obfervant nations, that finding the phrenzy of the French people increafed by our attack, we 'are determined no more to penetrate into the interior, or to employ direct or indirect means to oppofe it; but that we will wait the refult of this wonderful Revolution with the moft ardent defire that good may eventually be produced: but we can entertain no rational hopes that the increafe of intellect, the fource of all good, can be produced by any

thing

thing but civil difcipline accommodated to the powers of thought and reflection in the great mafs of the people, and calculated to fupprefs paffion, and liberate reafon, or difpaffionate inquiry, in a modified liberty of the prefs.

We conjure the French nation, in the facred names of Truth and Nature, to attempt the reeftablifhment of fyftem, which may organize the great mafs of population, fo as to give power to the will of the majority, and lay down fuch laws as may be adapted to the prefent human predicament with a capacity to improve into a graduated perfectability. We conjure them to reflect that all mankind are but fenfitive bubbles on the great ocean of matter, breaking and renovating by life and death, and that from the moral inftitutions of intellect the turbulency or tranquillity of that ocean is affected, which tranfmit good or evil to the identical diffolving and renovating matter revolving in the infeparable union of felf and nature to all eternity.

Were the above meafures to be purfued by the confederate powers, the fpring of the revolutionary power of France would be fo relaxed, that all its external efforts falling back upon its own center muft caufe a complete diffolution of all public authority, and France muft become a field of fuch atrocious and infufferable anarchy, that

that agonizing humanity would call upon furrounding nations for protection. If, on the con-
trary, order fhould miraculoufly be produced,
all nature would rejoice at fuch an event, as it
muft accelerate the æra of univerfal good.

A prefent view of the moral ftate of France
gives but little reafon to hope that the prefent
Revolution will caufe the progreffion, rather
than the retrogradation, of univerfal good. It
is not only involved in a chaos of practice, but
a chaos of theory alfo. Leaders of the moft
popular party expiring upon the fcaffold ; teachers of the moft popular opinions fhut up in pri-
fon ; patriots arrefted ; the altar of liberty co-
vered with mourning, to deter the inquiries of
juftice into the enormous peculation of fcoun-
drel demagogues ; virtue at fo low an ebb, that
the act of faving the life of an abandoned found-
ling is reported to the Convention and recorded
as a prodigy, and many other acts that in England are fo naturalized, that not to perform
them would expofe a man to public contempt,
are recorded in French annals as the phenomena
of private virtue.

Liften to the National Affembly debating
upon the confifcation of foreign property ; the
maximum of advantage was made the criterion
of their decifion ; no repugnance exprefled for
the

the dereliction of the facred principle of national faith and immutable juftice ; no modification
propofed which policy pleaded for, to grant a
fubfiftence to thofe creditors whofe property
united them to the profperity of France. The
watch-word was plunder, and detected their
lurking principle throughout the whole Revolution, to be the acquifition of property, and
the quick mode of transfer fubftituted to the
flow and unpleafant mode of induftry.

What a mark of plebeian folly does the late
decree (refpecting the emancipation of the flaves
in the iflands) betray ; this was done, they fay,
to fruftrate the plans of Pitt; a fchool-boy
would immediately have detected fo grofs an er-
ror ; this decree was equivalent to the furrender
of the iflands, and will change capitulation into
invitation. My heart fhudders while I find it
neceffary to reprehend fuch meafures of appa-
rent virtue ; but I know the character of the
people ; they do every thing by impulfe, and
nothing by reflection : they are fo fhort-fighted
and improvident that they never can fee the end,
but only the rule or means of action. The decree of emancipation will be the fiat of maffacre,
and the anarchy of the iflands will co-operate in
its own fimilitude with the anarchy of the me-
tropolis, to give a tremendous but important

D   leffon

leffon to mankind, that reafon and liberty muft
move in a parallel progreffion : liberty ever
fome few paces behind ; for any defultory ad-
vance muft have a recoil, whofe fudden weight
will caufe the retrogradation of both.

The thoughtleffnefs of the French character,
or averfion to contemplate propofitions till all
their relations are exhaufted, in the double ftate-
ment of predicament and perfectability, render
moral truth an ignis fatuus to miflead, and has
induced them to tranfmute the policy of thirty
millions of corrupt people, into a fraternity of
affimilated and innocent fectarians : the characteriftic vanity of the nation is become a fpring
of univerfal energy, while foreign enemies oppofe their delirium, and they would fuffer their
bodies to be reduced to inanition by famine in
the conteft, providing their fkins after death
were ftuffed by fame in the temple of vanity,
the Pantheon ; where nature, the integer of
exiftence, is rocked to fleep by the tranfmuta-
tion of its fractional parts in the opinion of
French philofophers.

I might produce a variety of inconteftable
facts to prove the moral character of the French
nation incompatible with the improvement of
civilization, and that nothing but defpotifm can
preferve them from total extirpation. A view
of

of the prefent ftate of the city of Lyons con-
centers every teftimony corroborative of this
fentiment. It is called *the enfranchifed city.*
According to the lateft reports, the troops of
the line had been fighting for three days and
three nights with the national guards. Eighty
thoufand inhabitants deprived of all means of
fubfiftence. The deftruction of Houfes. The
revolutionary tribunal with fpies and execution-
ers offering the only remedy of the fcaffold to
thofe whom hunger or the diftrefs of relatives
might caufe to figh or groan loud enough to be
heard. The afylum of civic virtue with its
doors fo enveloped in the fophiftry of Robefpe-
rian moderantifm, that no one can find its en-
trance placed between the extremes of fuperfti-
tion and atheifm, patriotifm and moderantifm.
Here then we have a view of the firft enfranchifed city, whofe code of rights terminates in
hunger and the fcaffold, and this paragon of
liberty and equality muft be followed by every
other city in France, when the confederate powers fhall have wifdom enough to declare a
peace, and thereby caufe the external energies
of France to recoil upon their own center.

Nothing but extreme thought and fenfibility
can make man provident of the end of action.
Short-fighted, unfeeling men enter upon the re-

volution

volution of a nation with the fame indifference
as the revolution of a dance, and they are difpofed to caft off the moft facred inftitutions
with the fame levity as they would caft off
two couple ; and fuch is the unhappy moral
ftate of the French nation, who, notwithftand-
ing all their ingenuity in the field of knowledge,
are far removed from wifdom, which can be
attained only by learning to think or to invert
the mind upon itfelf, the only operation which
can produce manhood.

Should the prefent war be continued upon an
offenfive fyftem, I predict the diffolution of fociety over all Europe, and its confequent fubjection to Afiatic tyrants. The energy of
France in proportion to the preffure, like a tube
of water, will overflow upon furrounding nations to refift its torrents, the great mafs of the
people muft be armed by their governments,
and the deftruction of all civil authority muft
enfue.

To enable Great Britain to outlive the general
wreck of civilization, I propofe the following
meafures to be purfued :—That a conftitutional
army be immediately formed of all men of property ; that the qualification of a volunteer be an
acre of land, a houfe, or £.500 fterling in ef-
fects ; thofe individuals whofe fum might ex-
ceed

ceed, should have the privilege to guarantee a volunteer for every exceeding sum of qualification he possesses, or 20 acres of land; that an oath should be administered to maintain the present constitution practically and theoretically, till the most evident majority of the people so qualified should testify their desire to reform it.

In Great Britain property is so generally diffused, that I have no doubt 3 or 400,000 men could be embodied, armed, and disciplined, which would secure this country from all internal or external assaults. The thoughtful, reflective character of Britons, the product of education through a series of ages, enables this country to view the very essence of the present revolutionary spirit, which aims at nothing but the acquisition of property by the substitution of transfer to industry. The defence of this island in such a contest can no longer be entrusted to mercenary and ignorant soldiers liable to the seduction of sophistry or interest, by whom subordination is at all times regarded as the greatest of all evils, and nothing but the fear of death holds them to their functions.

This constitutional army is to be called out by the king, and pay to be given to those who cannot subsist without it. The establishment alone of such an army would prevent the neces-

fity

lity of its being called forth; what troops dare mutiny, what infurgents dare affemble, what enemy dare invade, when they know the government of this country is fupported by 400,000 volunteer citizens affembled upon the firft fignal? Such an army would not only pre-ferve this ifland from the general wreck of ci-vilization, but would accelerate the progrefs of human perfectability by procuring a total eman-cipation of oral or written difcourfes; feditious fentiment would have no other effect than to provoke difcuffion and prepare the triumph of civic knowledge, without the aid of Heffians, a police of fpies, judicial fentences, or facts which bring to memory the fable of Hercules and the Carter, which, however expedient, have lately operated to excite the indignation, degrade the reafon, and debafe the civic character of the Bri-tifh nation.

When I take a comprehenfive view of the paft and prefent operations of the moral world, I am moft confidently of opinion that nothing but affumptive power can feparate the optimacy from the peffimacy of the people, or organize the mafs of a nation into the conftitutional fhape of head and body, with its feveral mem-bers. The active fovereignty of the people in populous nations can have no exiftence; the

prefent

prefent plebocracy of France muft terminate in fome democratical conftitution, whofe perpetual contention will draw all the efforts of the mind from felf-contemplation to the means of political, civil, and natural fubfiftence ; whofe broils keeping the mind in external operation, will never prefent that peaceful medium in which it is brought to invert upon itfelf and produce thought and reflection.

In the government of an optimacy, like the Britifh conftitution, fupported by the volunteer army before propofed, fociety is organized with a head and a body, and becomes a political entity or identified mode of being, by whofe unitary energy great paffions and great reafon is produced.

" Paffion is the Card, but Reafon is the Gale."

The vigour of induftry, encouraged by the honors of the ftate, prepares a fuperfluity which, overflowing upon the community, furnifhes an eafy fubfiftence to contemplative men, and produces that medium of leifure, peace, and competence, in which philofophy thrives and difcovers the progreffive nature of moral truth. The feverity of difcipline, moral, civil, and political, keeps the great mafs of the

3   people

people or body in due fubordination, while fac-
titious wants and defires increafe their fenfibility, and this their intellect, the fpring of all
perfectability.

Advocates for democracy miftake its turbulency for energy, and contentions of fubfiftence
for the progrefs of fentiment. The philofophers of Greece and Rome had no auditors, but
their pupils, and demagogues were the only
teachers of practical policy which abforbed all
moral principles; were it poffible for any of the
ancients to renovate in their former precife
identities and vifit this ifland, they would be
confounded to hear more noble fentiment and
true philofophy taught in toafts at a convivial
banquet, than was ever known in their academies of fophifticated nonfenfe, where founds
held the place of fenfe, and words of things;
and he who had the talent of talking or wri-
ting what was unintelligible to both himfelf and
others, was dubbed a philofopher.

When the conftitutional army fhall have been
embodied, organized, and difciplined, the æra
of public fafety will commence, and with it
the progrefs of moral, civil, and political perfectability, the corrupt fyftem of penfions and
finecure places may then be abolifhed; no hun-
gry oppofitionift would dare to oppofe the mea-

fures

fures of government, but upon the ground of public welfare : members of Parliament would become counfellors of the nation, and if their opinions failed to direct, their patriotic zeal would
ftill co-operate to execute the will of the majority.

The moral happinefs of the community would
then become the firft object of State Councils.
Academies might be formed like thofe of the
ancients, where philofophers might publicly
difcufs all propofitions which concerned human
perfectability ; committees of moral economy
might be eftablifhed to take cognizance of the
health, fubfiftence, and fports of the people ;
popular affociations might be formed to prefent
the accumulated energy of intellect againft every
domeftic evil that afflicted human fociety.

I fee but one evil which oppofes the Britifh
zenith of focial exiftence, and that is, the hete-
rogeneity of the great mafs of its fubjected population. In Ireland and Scotland, was a conftitutional army to take place before thought and
reflection had affimilated them more to the Britifh character, I fear the horrors of civil war in
thofe countries would oblige England to re-
eftablifh the Wall of Adrian, and cut off
thefe dependencies from the advantage of its
moral union, which would ftill remain the head

E   of

of the world, the protector of humanity, and the progreffive point of perfectability to all exiftence.

Ireland, through the extreme diffipation and ferocity of its inhabitants, produces nothing but victims of mifery and folly to weild the fword of Britifh conquefts; induftry, uncultivated and oppreffed, gives no fraternal aid to the laborious peafantry of Britain, ftaggering under the load of a national debt accumulated to purchafe a commerce which honeft Ireland would choofe to participate in profit, but not in lofs. If you afk contributary taxes, they fay they are poor; this excufe might ferve every diffipated drunken inhabitant of a parifh when the public collector calls upon him for payment. Why are they poor? Becaufe a want of thought makes them all men of pleafure from the duke to the beggar; commerce fails through a want of punctuality, induftry is deftroyed by the harpy hand of diffipation, which can afford no indulgence to an opprefled tenantry; in fhort, pleafure caufes fuch a morbid circulation of property in the body politic, that it is at all times in a fever which threatens a letiferous crifis, unlefs Britifh influence oppofed power to defect of thought as the only remedy to their incivic malady.

3   Scotland,

Scotland, though poffeffing a better moral character than Ireland, is ftill defective in civic virtue. Though punctuality gives uncommon vigour to their commerce, induftry is ftill checked by the cold hand of avarice in the land-holders, which freezes the blood of the labouring poor, and drives them for relief to the wages and livery of folly in the Britifh army. They pay taxes, indeed, to fupport the burthen of the public debt, but it is payed in fuch a proportion that ftigmatizes both their foil and their civifm. I fear a conftitutional army can take place in neither * Ireland or Scotland, 'till the martial character has been more pacified by commerce and agriculture, which introducing luxury, fows the feed of fenfibility ; and this the feverity of civil and domeftic difcipline meliorates into thought and reflection ; when thefe take place in the mind of the individual, the feed of perfectability is fown, which requires the education of fome

---

* In Ireland, the eftablifhment of a volunteer army which had not property for its bafis, had very near overturned the conftitution ; but no inference can be drawn from the example of an irreflective people, to deter a thoughtful people from a meafure fo effential to their fafety in the prefent dangerous predicament, when the very exiftence of focial order is threatened by internal and external enemies, and while the horrors of French anarchy prefents an antidote to the contagion of its example.

generations

generations to mature into the knowledge of
self, or true civism of existence;

> " For self and nature link'd in one great frame,
> " Proves true self-love, and social is the same.

These countries, like all the other parts of
the British dependencies, must be held in peace
by the influence of British power and British
wisdom, and should their connections become
disadvantageous or troublesome to Great Britain,
they might be thrown off as a load which checks
her career to that climax of moral, civil, political, and natural perfectability, which they must
inevitably attain if the establishments of a
constitutional army should take place, and
guard her line of progress from all hostile con-
tingencies.

To remove the censure of inconsistency
which will, no doubt, be heaped upon an author
who urges man to progress towards perfectability, and reproves him when he makes it, (I here
allude to Strictures on the Conduct of the French
Revolution, and its abettors in this Country.)
I will make the most ample confession of all the
inward operations of my mind; I love system,
and abhor contingency, not that the change
threatens the loss of comforts. I can live upon
potatoes, sleep upon straw, cloath myself in a
sheep's

sheep's skin; what loss of comforts then can
the uproar of revolution bring to me? I'll tell
you, the loss of mental liberty to speak all I
think; and as I think instructively and not in-
flammatorily, in a peaceful society this loss must
succeed to anarchy and uproar. You will
answer probably, yes, for a time, as the war
begets peace. To this I reply, when reformation in a state assumes a temperate and co-
ordinate predicament so as to give power a new
form, I should boldly face the momentary
anarchy it might threaten, and probable calculation of improvement would assure my
hopes of perfectability: but when I see the
social fabric attacked and overturned in its
very foundation, personal safety and personal
property, and this by a nation whose moral
character of levity and thoughtlessness is notorious, I am apalled, and I can see nothing but
barbarism preparing the grave of civilization,
contingency presenting a dreadful vortex to
overwhelm system, and despotism implored to
save the annihilation of the human species by
the total extinction of human wisdom.

I hold a long lease in my tenement of existence, and seek no rack-rent operations; I believe my interest inseparable and eternal with
the whole mass of matter, of which I must ever

form

form a component part, that whatever may be its various modifications of energies, they are beyond the reach of ken and communication. Every fphere can take cognizance only of its own independent energy, by the exercife of which its own fphere being improved, all intervolving matter muft be benefitted in time and eternity : I feek only the progrefs of human energy or intellect, and believe that to be the beft fyftem of government which has power to reftrain paffion and liberate thought; and fuch is the Britifh Government practically and theoretically.

I conjure the adminiftration of this country to look with anxious contemplation on this awful crifis, and while a neighbouring nation, ftruck with a martial frenzy (the offspring of their natural levity ftimulated by invafion) is arming the whole of its inhabitants ; is it wife for Britain to fleep behind its wooden walls, guarded by mercenary armies of plebeians inadequate to protection in the new civil predicament of nations ; when the poor are incited to plunder the rich by a fyftem of equality, which none but fools can learn, or knaves can teach, and which would bring fuch an univerfal contention of paffions among the human fpecies, that nothing but the moft cruel defpotifm could check, in which reason or perfectability must retrograde to an incalculable distance ?

Before I conclude this epitome of discussion upon so awful a crisis, I shall endeavour to concentre all reflections and relations upon the subject of civil society into a point, and present a most important question for the contemplation of the public mind, viz. which is the best form of government in the present predicament of mankind, to protect and promote the increase of human intellect, the source of all perfectability ?

In my travels over the most populous and most interesting parts of the globe, I have always observed knowledge bore a parallel progress with the energies of government. I shall begin eastward with China ; in this country, where kingly power is at its zenith, the arts and sciences are in a most pre-eminent progress relative to other eastern countries. In India and Tartary, the progress of science has universally ceased, but their books and histories furnish evidence of the past progress of science in a parallel with the peaceful dynasties of their powerful kings. In Persia, their libraries which now exist, have had no augmentation since the expulsion of kingly power, and the succession of contending rebel chiefs
exercising

exercising a precarious and very limited authority. In Turkey, the Sultan has made several attempts to establish a press for the circulation of science, but insurrection of the people which keeps the throne perpetually vacillating, threatened to tear the hand that offered it food, and sovereign power was obliged to indulge them with the darkness they preferred to light. In Germany, the dispersion of light and science was graduated by the balance of power, between the sceptre and the mitre. The Emperor had established the freedom of the press, but the power of superstition at last triumphed, and it was supposed he was poisoned by the priesthood. In Italy, we see the progress of science marked by the power of the prince as in Tuscany. In France, the progress of science began with the most arbitrary of its princes, and has moved on in progression to the æra of the present anarchy, when nobody has leisure to write a book or inclination to read it, and the whole of the intellectual faculties are absorbed by fear, by political contention for power, or means for subsistence. We come at last to the extremity of the west, where we find a country where government nicely balanced and poised upon the hearts of the great majority of its people,

liberates

liberates the operations of thought, and re-
stricts those of passion, left precipitate action
might disturb the equilibre of a magic
constitution, the work of ages, and the wonder
of the world; but when a constitutional army
shall be established to guard the scales of power, the press will have a total liberation, and
the great question of which form of government can best protect intellect, will be answer-
ed by pointing to the British Government, the
paragon of civil polity.

The novelty and magnitude of a constitutional
armament, will, no doubt, appall the partizans
of antiquated laws and customs, but let them
reflect, that should French transports, protected
by red hot shot, land 100,000 ruffians, reeking
with the blood of their fellow citizens, to meet
only a bloodless troop of rustics, whom they
might fascinate with the caballa of liberty and
equality; what would be the fate of Britain?
Who can doubt a moment whether it is better
to trust the government of this country to a
constitutional army of Britons, or to submit it
to the mercy or the fraternity of sans culotte
conquerors.

As I wish much to imprefs the public with
a favourable opinion of my impartiality and
integrity, having confessed the state of my
mind, I will also expose the condition of

F   my

my perfon. * I have an annuity of 300l. per annum on my life in the French funds, which I purchafed ten years ago, (at 10 per cent. having vainly endeavoured to procure 8 per cent. in England) and which is now fufpended ; I have 500l. in the American funds, and 300l. in the Englifh funds. † I have lately applied to adminiftration to ferve this country as Oriental Interpreter ; I was anfwered that an alien was appointed for the important and fecret negotiations of the Turkifh Embaffy, and fince my application fome Oriental Embaffadors have been fent from the Secretary of State's office to the India Houfe, to procure an interpretation from the very people they bring complaints againft. Withered be the hand, and paralized be the heart, of that man whofe private intereft fhall dictate his public fentiments.

I am engaged in the caufe of truth and univerfal good, to which end, all rule of

---

* I was formerly in the fervice of the Eaft India Company, which I left becaufe I defpifed it; and travelled into the interior parts of India, to obtain that knowlege which might forward my great and only object, the good of nations and the good of nature, which defign was evinced by a letter wrote at the age of 18 years, and now upon the Company's record.

† All the above property was faved from mere falary, as Interpreter to fome Eaftern Princes, whofe fervice I quitted upon the acquifition of the above competency.

principle

principle muft bend, and all mode of action be
directed. I will flatter neither nations nor
minifters; let them throw their fops to the
Cerberi of faction; they can neither ftop nor
inflate my lungs, which are devoted to my
higher intereft of univerfal good. I hate your
fmiling affable complying demagogues; let
Pitt preferve his frowns, Grenville his pride,
Dundas his firmnefs, and they will fortify my
expectations of a fuccefsful adminiftration from
their united efforts in this moft awful and cri-
tical conjuncture, when the diffolution of civil
difcipline threatens to bring on the retrogradation of human perfectability.

Before I conclude, I muft congratulate my
country upon the prefent appearance of a moft
aufpicious moral phænomenon, which is the
alliance of patriotifm and power, brought about
by the audacity and atrocity of almoft every
defcription of oppofitionifts; parliamentary demagogues, appearing as advocates for the
enemy in their fophifticated orations, reform-
ing focieties in the correfpondence of inflammatory hand-bills, endeavouring to recall the
plebeian legiflation of Lord George Gordon;
the proftituted mifcreant editors of public
papers, promulgating paragraphs calculated to
convey intelligence to the foe, and to confound

all

all principles of civic virtue, and this tripartite union of unprincipled oppofition, fo openly manifefted againft all civil difcipline, ferves but to increafe the confternation of thoughtful citizens, and force them to join the ftandard of power to defend the ramparts of focial exiftence.

There is another clafs of oppofitionifts, which I muft mention apart from the reft, not that they are feparated from the general coalition of the enemies of Great Britain, but as they are the moft dangerous they muft be rendered the moft confpicuous tools of faction ; I mean the puritanical fect called diffenters, or prefbyterians: thefe madmen are fo endoctrined by their hypocritical paftors, that the peace, the inftitutions, and happinefs of this life, are all in contraft with thofe of future exiftence ; hence their enmity to all civil order which confines them to the precincts of a wholefome Bedlam of disfranchifements, to prevent the contagion of their dangerous enthufiafm.

The pages of univerfal hiftory are but fections of indictment of thefe hornets of the hive, they have ever been the fpring, the conduct, and the accomplifhment of all convulfive revolutions: they have ever played the parts of

rationicides

rationicides to let man loose in the career of superstition, ideotism, and credulity. The sceptics who endeavour to check fanaticism in this mad career, must support civil and political power, and if folly maintains the diminution of good in this life to be the augmentation of it in another, wisdom has a right to oppose such chimerical opinions, and by maintaining that the same perfect or imperfect state of the whole of existence in which man or matter dissolves, must be the very identical state in which he or it is to renovate, and thereby invite man to be the friend and supporter of such civil discipline, as in conforming to this nature by graduating perfectability may combine individual and universal, temporal and eternal good.

I must conclude this short view, this multum in parvo, with the following consolatory prediction : That should Great Britain be able to preserve her present constitution, practically and theoretically, by means of a constitutional army and the liberty of the press, guarded by virtuous Jurymen, the æra of truth over all the world, or the salvation of nature, will commence before the lapse of another century.

The most exalted efforts of human understanding have lately issued from the Eng-

lish

lifh prefs; fuch works as may, like the ferpent * Venom, poifon every nation but itfelf in poffeffion of the antidote. Thought, which difcriminates theory from practice, or predicament from perfectability; works calculated to difcourage action, and unite reflection, juft criterions of the pre-eminence of the Britifh Government, whofe nice poifed power folves the problem of civil difcipline, fuppreffing paffion and liberating reafon.

CONSIDERATIONS on PROPERTY.

PROPERTY of Kings and perfons feems the center on which civilization revolves : man muft be the head of his family, and the proprietor of their induftry, or the individual wheel would have no clog to receive an impulfe from the larger wheels in the grand machine of univerfal fociety.

Property is alfo the great fource of optimacy, its acquifition demanding all the energies of intellect, and furnifhing that medium of

* The fudden blaze of meridian truth may be as injurious to weak minds, as the light of the fun to feeble and morbid eyes. The defpotic governments on the Continent of Europe will form a falutary medium to refract the light of Britifh reafon, which muft pervade the whole Earth.

leifure

leisure by which its progress is made; it may be here objected, that poverty has oftener engendered philosophy, than riches; this is a most egregious mistake, occasioned by the use of words property, and mediocrity, as synonimous: there can be no study where the means of subsistence are absent, or where they are not assured by the laws of property, or meum and teum.

The desire of accumulating property, is the wind which preserves the ocean of intellectuality from putridity or stagnation; luxury engenders sensibility, and sensibility engenders thought and reflection, the only medium through which progressive truth or perfectability can be discovered. Men of learning and science have perpetually dealt out much common-place satire upon the evils of luxury; it is the peculiar province of genius alone, like fire, to separate drofs from the pure ore, and extract good from its ever concomitant evil.

In the present unenlightened state of the moral world, the most perfect community or nation is that in which property is most generally diffused, forming thereby a powerful minority of population that may be able to subject the great supplemental mass of the majority, and

and thereby conftitute the mode of fociety into head and members, like the human body, whofe greater members are fubordinate to the leffer head.

"Till the revelation of moral truth fhall appear, and the reign of reafon commence in the univerfal knowledge of felf and its unity with nature, affumptive power can alone form a happy coercion to human infanity; delegated power or univerfal reprefentation deftroys the unity and fupremacy of authority, and can ferve only as a moral to the ancient fable of the quarrel of the head and members of the human body, which muft take place over all the world whenever the bafis of property is fuddenly or violently annihilated.

In the prefent predicament of civilization, affumptive power is focial life, attacked by internal and external ignorance or violence, and it is ftrong in proportion to the number of its conftituent parts, and grows with their increafe, and national perfectability advances in a parallel ratio. The augmentation of property and power forms the fcale of national energy; philofophers, fectarians, and colonifts, under its ample protection, may develope new theories and practice of civilization, which, like the fapling, draws all the nutrition from its

parent

parent oak, and when its protecting branches become an impediment to its nurseling, the dissolution of the oak marks the prosperity of the sapling, and the whole world will become the colony of perfectable manhood.

If these admonitory sheets should not produce the salutary and indispensable measure of a constitutional army, and that the ancient military establishment of plebeian mercenaries shall be judged sufficient for defence in the new predicament or war of property, I shall retire to America, to save the germ of perfectability, unbiassed intellect, from the universal wreck which threatens civilization, and employ it to direct the Western Continent in its present moral infancy, while i should deplore the inconsolable loss of improving manhood in the too confident Island of Great Britain.

My reason has been long poising the scales of civil government, and has at length adjusted the weights; the scales are formed by assumptive and delegated authority, or aristocracy and democracy; the weights, power, and ignorance; when ignorance is ponderous in the latter, power must be counterpoised in the former; this gives a just energy to assumptive authority to restrain the passions, while delegated authority liberates the reason; and

G   since

fince the invention of the prefs nothing is wanting to affure progrefs to perfectability, but the fecurity of civil difcipline, adapted to the moral temperament of the people; if this fhould be loft, the world muft fall back into its priftine ftate of evil and ignorance.

I wifh to fay a few words more before I conclude to anticipate objections, which may be made to the conftitutional armament, as promoting difcriminations which may create a jealoufy between men of property and thofe of no property; fuch objections are already anfwered by the purport of all civil qualifications, which has eftablifhed government upon the bafis of fuch difcrimination. The poor themfelves, if they poffefs the leaft fhare of reafon, muft be intuitively fenfible that their induftry is protected by civil difcipline as much as property, and whenever anarchy arrives, the induftry of the poor muft be its firft victim.

Let the poor beware of the infatuating doctrine of the *Rights of Man*, the war whoop of faction. Rights of legality are applicable to man in his domeftic ftate alone, but in his political ftate right muft be applicable to rectitude, and not legality of action; and public fafety, though fenced in by legal rights to keep out faction, muft have its portals wide open

for

for patriotifm, moving on the flexible line of rule and means to principle, the goal of general good.

I have for feveral years paft been contemplating the momentous queftion of government, or that form of civil difcipline which may beft promote and protect the higheft energy of this fphere of exiftence, human intellect; and I have at length decided in favour of affumptive power adapted to the ignorance of the fubject people, under whofe wing philofophy muft have progrefs, either creeping or walking erect in the fecret or public efforts of the prefs; univerfal delegated power muft bring on anarchy in populous and luxurious empires, and apathy in fmall and ruftic ftates, till truth and reafon fhall have been more generally diffufed amongft mankind.

I know that defpotifm is as hoftile as anarchy to philofophy; but as the fecret efforts of the prefs can no more be extinguifhed than the rays of the fun, intellect muft have progrefs, however flow; power is to the politic body, what refpiration is to the human body, when difeafe takes place in either, from want of regimen in the head; fhould the members refufe their obedient functions, diffolution muft take place; but while life continues, remedy may be hoped for from the head, and nothing but dan-

gerous

gerous motion can derive from the members of either body.

Objections may be made to the above allegory by incompatible references to the Grecian, Roman, and British government; these, however, present nothing but the modifications of assumptive power. The helots, slaves, and disfranchised peasants, claimed no interference; but the present turbulent spirit of revolution would confound the base of the pyramid with its vertex, and place power in the hands, not of property, but number; not in the head alone, but in all the members of the politic body; this novel, dangerous, and incongruous system should form the tocsin of the world, and drive all reflective people to join the standard of power to preserve civilization from universal chaos, and the energy of intellect, the cause of all good to the unity of self and nature in time and eternity, from revolving back to barbarism and total darkness.

I have been the first agent in my philosophic works to couch the mental eye of man, and it behoves me to attemper the medium of vision to restored sight. I have been the first to increase the measure of perfectability, that quality which alone distinguishes the human from the brutal species; it behoves me peculiarly to procure

procure its germination in the climate of reafon, and check its pullulation in the hot-bed of
paffion, and for this purpofe to promulgate the
following confummate political maxim over all
the world. That the bafe of focial energy is
a capacity to reftrain paffion and liberate reafon, and that its vertex is a great mafs of optimacy or thoughtful citizens forming a conftitutional army to confolidate the pyramid of fociety, cemented by the fafety of perfon and property, of which maxim the Britifh conftitution will, I hope, foon become an illuftrious
criterion.

Ere my Tocfin ceafes to toll, let its dying
ofcillations bear the following apology for my
fudden change from temperate reformer to zealous alarmift. The conduct of the Houfe of
Lords upon the Heffian bufinefs, at a period
when titles, property, and privilege is at iffue,
has feduced my confidence in Britifh ariftocracy, while inflammatory hand-bills diftributed
to the populace by demagogues at a period
when focial exiftence is in jeopardy, has dif-
gufted me with democracy. The pompous
banner of fentimental theory under which
French democrats urge the giddy mob to general plunder, never dazzled my eyes; I know
their characteriftic diffimulation, and I know

that

that fhould their animal courage (or difeftima-
tion of life) enable them to fubdue the world,
that fame quality of thoughtleffnefs or irreflection muft ultimately deftroy themfelves.

One clangorous peal more and then let the
curfew ceafe: I call upon Government to *arm
men of property, to arm them inftantaneoufly,
and let all thoughtful men of induftry join to fave
the focial fabric from deftruction,* and then I
will again ftep forward and become a moft
zealous reformift to defend the characteriftic
fenfibility of the Englifh plebacy from fuffe-
rance, and the thought of optimacy from er-
ror. O Britons! think and deliberate with
freedom upon all fubjects in domeftic focieties,
the true medium of fair difquifition. Who
calls you to affemble or to action, means to
miflead you with eloquence (difquifition is incompatible with multitude) he is your enemy,
the enemy of England, of focial exiftence, and
of all nature.

I was the firft to difcover the perfectability
of human nature, and I will labour to mark out
the defcent from the precipices of civilization
by the fafe road of a gradual reform in the protective and powerful energy of civil difcipline.

CONCLUSION.

I FEAR I have undertaken the tafk of the travelled Laplander, who, upon his return to his countrymen, endeavoured to perfuade them they were the fhorteft men in the world, or pigmies. They obferved to him in anfwer, that they had fhort men of three feet, and tall men of four feet, and that they difclaimed the name of pigmies, which might be applicable to the whole world as well as themfelves.

I wifh to perfuade the Englifh people that they are the happieft, the wifeft, the moft powerful, and beft governed of any other over the whole globe : I may be anfwered, that in England there is mifery, folly, political debility, and corruption. Yes, of thefe truths I am very fenfible ; but as the perfection of one individual is to be difcovered only by a comparifon with another, fo it is with nations, whofe comparifon muft ever be fought out of themfelves.

I appeal folely to travellers of obfervation, whether on the road or in the library, to bear teftimony to my following declarations ; that

in

in no country except England, is the subsistence of poverty provided for by poor laws; in no country but England is education so generally diffused as to establish a mass of moral excellence, producing liberal protection and manly subordination, the pendulum of the social machine; in no country but England is justice administered with unsuspected integrity; in no country but England is property circulated with that liberal currency which gives life to industry; (an Englishman would close the bargain for the purchase of a house, before a foreigner would finish his higgling for an egg) in no country but England is religious worship administered to improve the internal moral energies of the human sphere, and restrict superstition from confounding them with the passive and incommunicable energies of unknown spheres; in no country but England is the political government so magically organized, that its very imperfections are its energies to conduct ignorant manhood through the tortuous mutability of predicament on to the graduated line of perfectability; and I am most conscientiously of opinion, that the English government, domestic, civic, and politic, is the only medium in which human perfectability can have progress, and that whatever may

may be the revolutions or changes of power
amongſt nations, they muſt ultimately attain
the point of mixed government as in England,
before they will deſerve the names of conſtitution, or promiſe any permanent ſyſtem accommodated to the improvement of manhood. Let
us then not only as Engliſhmen, but as men,
ſenſible of our unity with nature in time and
eternity, join hand and heart to defend that
country on whoſe decadence or proſperity de-
pends the progreſs or retrogreſs of all moral
perfectability.

Having for a long period revolved in my
mind the ſubject of ſocial organization, I have
formed the following mature, concluſive, and
comprehenſive opinion:—that the progreſs of
humanization muſt be made through the corrupt medium of luxury and refinement, and the
progreſs of civilization through the corrupt and
contentious medium of mixed government;
and through this double medium muſt be produced the colony of manhood, or ſtate of enlightened nature : here human * perfectability

---

* The colony of manhood will produce ſuch profound peace
and ſtagnation of paſſion, that wiſdom will putrefy and diſſolve
into ignorance, when moral motion will repeat its cycle of diſ-
ſolution and renovation like all other parts of exiſtence.

H   muſt

muft culminate and revolve eternally in this tripartite cycle.

Let me afk the democrats or reformers, what it is they wifh, or what they are attempting to achieve; fubjects of a country that alone merits the name of a nation? Do they wifh it wifer, richer, happier, or more powerful? then let them unite in private focieties, and by difpaffionately inveftigating truth, let them improve the moral character of the thinking part of their fellow citizens; but if by inflammatory hand-bills they ftimulate to action the thoughtlefs labourer or mechanic, they will but excite mutiny in the veffel of the ftate, labouring through the prefent ftorm of policy, and all muft be loft.

Could we judge of their intentions by the declaration of their high-prieft, Tom Paine, they wifh for a cheap government. America has, indeed, a government fo cheap, that it is trampled under feet by all rival nations, againft whom it affords not the energies of protection, and internally has no power to enforce obedience to its civil laws. The government of England is, no doubt, dear bought, but then it holds the dominion of the ocean in appanage; it procures for its travelling fubjects the refpect of fovereigns; its man-

date

date gives peace or war to the whole world, and its menaces alone saved the Turkish Empire from the victorious arms of confederated Europe. France has a very cheap government; but unfortunately, it has so little internal energy, that it cannot procure subsistence for its citizens, or assure freedom even to the high-priest of liberty, who is now in prison; and should the sans culotte conquerors triumph over this country, the most enraged English democrat would make but cheap food for the French guillotine. I know those men the readiest disposed to action, are ever possessed of the least share of thought and reflection, and I fear my Tocsin will rather impel than restrain them; but I have the most sanguine hopes that it will assemble together all men of thought and property under the standard of government, and that by measures of energetic expediency and patriotic Jurymen, the fanaticism of democrats (insects of contingency) may be impeded from creating a mutiny in the crew, and that the vessel of Britannia may become the ark of civilization, and save it from the universal deluge of licentious liberty and equality, which now threatens the moral world.

I am the democrat of nature, and view the perfectability of manhood at its most elevated

point,

point, on the fcale of intellect (where the optics of the political democrat cannot reach) but I look down at the fame time to the low point of predicament, and thought gives me fagacity to graduate the fcale of union; and when a con-ftitutional armament fhall have placed props to the fabric of the conftitution, to guard it from the outrage of fanatical innovation, I will then boldly and confidently work hard to repair it, as the only matrix or afylum of the higheft comprehenfible and final energy of exiftence of this fphere, progreffive intellect.

HAND BILL,

FOR THE

PLEBEIAN CLASSES OF THE COMMUNITY,

Recommended to wealthy Patriots, to print and circulate over all England.

POOR and induſtrious fellow countrymen, beware of an artful, cunning claſs of men, who call themſelves patriots, and go about with inflammatory diſcourſe and ſeditious writings, to wean your love from the Britiſh Conſtitution, which has for many ages raiſed your condition of peace, plenty, and liberty, to be envied by the enſlaved and miſerable poor of all other nations. They impoſe upon you by long harangues when you are aſſembled, and ſeduce you with the flattering words of liberty and equality, to change the preſent form of government, where power is reſponſible, for one in which you could have no ſhare, and they would have all the profit without any reſponſibility.

Examine

Examine the character of thefe patriots, you will find the moſt part of them diſſipated, thoughtleſs rakes, who, having no powers of reaſon to give happineſs to themſelves, feek to be appointed by you, the guardians of the public happineſs. You know well enough by your own experience, that the man who ſpends all his week's labour at the alehouſe, can never govern well his family; and how many are obliged to give their money to their wives, that they may have no liberty to fpend it. How few men know how to govern their own ſelves or families where all is ſimple, to procure health and ſubſiſtence for their own perſons; what would theſe men do with the great family of the nation, where matters are ſo difficult and complicated, that wiſdom itſelf is puzzled with the taſk !

You are exactly to the nation, what the arms and legs are to the body; if this is ſick, the head alone can keep a diet to effect a cure; if the arms and legs were to govern, they would carry the body into the open air, and ſo deſtroy it; juſt ſo muſt be your interference with the policy of the nation, nothing but diſorder could enſue, and induſtry and property muſt firſt feel the pain of national ſickneſs.

When

When these thoughtless rioting patriots talk
to you of liberty and equality, would the in-
dustrious and ingenious artist, who earns three
or five shillings a day, divide it with the idle
or ignorant, who can earn but a shilling?
would the weak bodied and weak spirited men
with the robust and angry to have more liberty and less law? then must follow the state of
French brotherhood, where property is so equally divided, that nobody has any thing to eat,
and the liberty of complaining is followed close
by the guillotine.

Be advised by an honest man, who formerly subsisted upon property, but must in
future depend upon his industry; envy not
the condition of the rich, who riot in gluttony
and voluptuousness; disease, vexation, and
insupportable melancholy are their companions.
You toil, but that procures you health, tranquillity, and cheerfulness. The landlord of the
soil whose heart is bursting with care and dif-
ease, in his gilded chamber, would give all
his property to enjoy the health and cheerfulness of his servants in the humble, but jovial
kitchen.

Read, teach your children to read; con-
verse frequently with one another on all sub-
jects, but listen to no harangues of public
orators;

orators ; they wifh only to render your inno-
cence, ignorance, and induftry, the victims of
their thoughtlefs ambition, that feeks to deftroy
all order, to make a play-field for their reftlefs
difpofitions : whenever they accoft you with
their treacherous inftruction, tell them you
are determined to follow the Yeomanry of the
country ; that clafs juft above you in the community, who have education, and underftand-
ing to judge better than you of what evil muft
be borne, and what may be remedied ; that on
them you place all your confidence, as from
their commerce your induftry draws all its fupport, and that you are determined never to
act till you are capable firft to underftand,
left you fhould be engaged in the broils of a
drunken club, where the candles being knocked
out, friends beat friends in the dark, and
general confufion enfues, in which all the
membrs are equally injured or deftroyed.

FINIS.

www.ingramcontent.com/pod-product-compliance
Lightning Source LLC
Chambersburg PA
CBHW021229260626
47172CB00002B/675

* 9 7 8 3 3 3 7 0 6 4 6 6 2 *